MYSTERIOUS CHRISTMAS

CONNOR WHITELEY

No part of this book may be reproduced in any form or by any electronic or mechanical means. Including information storage, and retrieval systems, without written permission from the author except for the use of brief quotations in a book review.

This book is NOT legal, professional, medical, financial or any type of official advice.

Any questions about the book, rights licensing, or to contact the author, please email connorwhiteley@connorwhiteley.net

Copyright © 2024 CONNOR WHITELEY

All rights reserved.

DEDICATION
Thank you to all my readers without you I couldn't do what I love.

INVITATION TO SECRETS, LIES AND DECEIT

2nd December 2022

Canterbury, England

No one thinks about the walls.

Before Private Eye Bettie English had fallen in love, before she had become President of The British Private Eye Federation and before she had given birth to two amazing kids, Bettie actually got a lot of cases through strange invitations. Hell, she loved it and she had gotten some of her best and most exciting cases from invitations from mystery senders.

But as she sat at a massive oak round table with only four other people she was really starting to regret her joy of receiving weird invitations.

The dining room she sat in was rather nice and almost magical in a way with beautiful red, green and bright pink tinsel hanging all over the walls and ceiling and the tinsel shined like stars off the crystal chandelier (that was probably real), Bettie had seen some impressive families do great on their Christmas decorations but this family might have topped it.

There of course wasn't one or two or even three massive pine trees in the dining room, there was one in each corner. And Bettie was amazed that each Christmas tree was decorated in an identical way with rainbow coloured LED lights gently pulsing Christmas magic, golden tinsel hugging the tree loosely and little naked candles burning on the trees filling the air with the sweet scents of frankincense and myrrh.

Bettie wasn't exactly sure why the hell these four people wanted to burn naked candles on their trees (surely they knew that was a fiery death sentence) but Bettie didn't really want to argue.

Not when she had received a very panicked letter two hours ago wanting her to attend because someone was going to die tonight.

Bettie had originally planned to spend the night with her amazing, sexy boyfriend Graham as they went through all the great (and utterly rubbish) Christmas decorations that her 70-year-old mum had given her and then Bettie was going to read her two little angels a Christmas bedtime story before she put them to bed (but them sleeping when she wanted them to was a joke at this moment. Four-month-old babies didn't like sleeping).

But the invitation had changed those plans in a flash.

"Welcome everyone," the very tall woman,

probably 32, at the head of the table said with a massive smile.

Bettie rather liked the woman's blue jeans, white shirt and shoeless feet, because it made her look normal and calm and like she was there to make sure everyone had a good time. It was just a shame that the other people at the table didn't look like that.

The other three people at the table were tall middle-aged men and wow did they look the part, and not the good or normal part, the three men were dressed in what Bettie could only describe as "grandad clothes" with their tan slacks, monocle and knitted red jumpers that looked so old they were about to fall apart.

Bettie was looking forward to seeing what these people were meeting about, and most importantly who was going to die. Something Bettie was hoping beyond hope that she could stop.

"We all know why we are here tonight," the tall woman said. "Three years ago, my father Lord Admiral Collins of the British Royal navy disappeared,"

"Happy Collins Day," the three men returned.

Bettie was shocked that she was actually attending Collins Day. She had read about it in the paper recently because his daughter, Beatrice and presumably the tall woman was her, had been launching new campaigns in search of information about her father's disappearance.

Bettie had even had a crack at the case whilst she

was on maternity leave during those extremely precious moments when her beautiful angels were finally sleeping.

The case was as strange as it got. Mr Collins had been on leave from the Navy for a month because Beatrice was getting married to the love of her life and Collins wanted to be there for the wedding and Christmas and New Year.

So he left the Naval Base at Portsmouth, England and drove to Canterbury two hours away, he kissed his wife hello and quickly popped to the shops to get some wine to celebrate his return (that was his wife's idea) and then he was never seen again.

There were no witnesses, no security footage that saw him on the second of December 2019 and his wife never heard from him again.

"Beatrice," Bettie said leaning forward, "why did your mother not get the wine?"

Everyone just looked at Bettie like she was a crazy woman.

"Who are you?" the oldest of the three men asked and Bettie noticed a minor scar under his chin like he had been punched there.

"This is Bettie English, the best private eye in the UK and somehow *she* received an invitation tonight," Beatrice said.

Bettie forced herself not to seem surprised at that comment. She was sure that if anyone had requested her presence tonight it would be Beatrice, but she certainly didn't invite Bettie with *that* tone.

"My question," Bettie said again, not really caring for the group's concern towards her.

"My mother was a woman in her late fifties who had just broken her leg after she fell down the stairs. She could barely let my father into the house let alone getting some wine," Beatrice said.

Bettie slowly nodded. That made sense.

"Nibbles Mrs Collins," a man said behind Bettie.

Bettie turned around and smiled when a very young man, maybe 19, walked in wearing a black waiter's uniform carrying a large silver tray of wine, freshly roasted nuts and smoked salmon.

Bettie loved all of those things but one part of herself she had never gotten back after her pregnancy was the ability to eat animal products. Bettie forced herself not to react to the amazing smell of the salmon despite her stomach churning.

Clearly these people didn't know about the possible death threat as the waiter placed the wine and nuts and salmon on the table and then bought out five silver plates and cutlery for them to enjoy the salmon on.

Bettie was starting to wonder if the person who actually invited her was really at the table.

"Are you not drinking Miss English?" the waiter said with concern edging his voice.

"No thank you," Bettie said. "I'm driving and I have two kids at home so I don't anymore,"

"Oh please Bettie," Beatrice said. "This wine is from the hills of Southern France, an area that my father loved. This is how we honour him on Collins Day,"

Bettie politely nodded and pretended to take a sip or two but she did not. The waiter just smiled at her and Bettie was almost a little concerned that everyone wanted her to drink. What if there was poison or something in the wine?

"What have you discovered about my father?" Beatrice asked the three men.

The youngest of the middle-aged man who Bettie was only realising now had a black eye smiled at Beatrice.

"We found one person who remembers selling your father a bottle of wine on the night in question," he said.

Bettie leant forward. "How? I didn't think the Police or Military police found anyone,"

The man with the scar under his chin sighed. "It's a great shame of our society that time loosen up tongues a lot better than a murder,"

Don't say that," Beatrice said. "My father is not dead,"

"My apologies Mrs Collins,"

That was a strange comment and now Bettie was seriously starting to wonder how the hell these people all knew each other. Bettie had believed they were friends or something but surely friends use first names and not formal surnames?

Beatrice started coughing a little and holding her stomach.

"Are you okay?" Bettie asked standing up.

Beatrice took a sip of the wine and smiled as she started picking at her salmon a little.

Bettie really wasn't liking this situation at all. She felt like a fish out of water but the mother angle was still annoying Bettie.

"Beatrice," Bettie said, "is this the same house that your mother lived in all those years ago?"

Beatrice coughed a little more and nodded before picking up a massive chunk of flaky salmon and eating it.

Bettie paced around the wooden table a little. "I assume your mother would have been in here with similar decorations when your father rang the doorbell,"

"Of course," Beatrice said grinning. "These are even the exact same decorations that were up on the night of the disappearance,"

Bettie almost felt sorry for Beatrice because she was clearly so obsessed with finding what happened to her father that Bettie was concerned she didn't have much of a life outside this hunt for the truth.

If Beatrice's mother had told the truth to the police then there was another problem, if she really had broken her leg and was on crutches then Bettie had to admit the mother was strong to walk herself all the way to the front door.

"I hadn't focused on it before," Bettie said, "but your dining room is at the back of the house and you cannot walk straight through the hallway to get from the front door to the dining room,"

Beatrice slammed her fork down on the table.

"You have to go through a number of other rooms with lots of twists and turns and this house probably has tons of hollow walls. If your mother really did that then why wasn't she more tired? And where was the waiter?"

The three men looked at Beatrice and nodded.

"You seem to be obsessed with keeping everything the same so there had to be a waiter, probably the same waiter, three years ago. Why didn't he answer the door? Or better yet, why didn't your father open the door with his front door keys?"

Beatrice downed her wine in a single gulp. "I don't know damn you. I don't know what happened to my father. I don't know what happened to my mother that night. I don't know anything,"

Bettie went over to her and folded her arms. "What do you mean you don't know what happened to your mother that night? Did she lie to the police?"

All three men stood up and went over to Beatrice. Their arms folded.

Beatrice held her stomach a little tighter. "My mother was out that night. She texted my father saying she would be home soon so he went to get the wine as a surprise,"

Bettie looked at the men. "She was having an affair, wasn't she?"

"No. No. No," Beatrice said. "That ain't true. My mummy was not having an affair,"

The last of the men that Bettie hadn't focused at all on yet just looked to the ground. And Bettie noticed his massive balding patch.

"How long did you sleep with her mother?" Bettie asked calmly.

Beatrice folded her arms and looked like she was about to cry.

"I didn't mean to sleep with her," he said not daring to look up. "I didn't mean to have sex with her. I didn't mean, well, any of it,"

Beatrice hissed a little.

"It was just my wife left me years ago, your mother was so nice and she was annoyed at the Navy for always taking her husband away from her. We were both lonely," he said.

"Damn you Jasper," Beatrice said.

Bettie went over to Jasper and gently raised his head with a single finger. "Did you kill Mr Collins?"

Jasper didn't even smile like that was a stupid thing to say, instead he simply shook his head as his eyes turned wet and Bettie knew, really knew that he was telling the truth.

Someone collapsed to the ground.

Bettie spun around.

The man with the black eye was gasping for air.

Bettie laid him perfectly straight, tried for a pulse and she didn't find one.

"Call an ambulance!" Bettie shouted.

Bettie immediately started CPR as hard and fast as she could.

Moments later the man gasped as air rushed into his lungs but he didn't open his eyes or move. But he was breathing and for now that would have to do.

Bettie picked him up and placed him gently back into his chair allowing him to lay unconscious, with his head tilted to one side so in case he vomited he wouldn't choke on it.

"I called an ambulance. They'll be here in the next hour," Beatrice said.

Bettie laughed because that really was a testament to how bad the ambulance service was getting in the UK.

"What's going on?" Jasper asked.

Bettie looked at the half-eaten plates of salmon plus her own intact plate and Bettie shook her head.

The food had to be poisoned but it also made no sense. Why poison that particular man? Why not poison Jasper or Beatrice or even herself?

Hell maybe they had poisoned Bettie.

"The waiter," Bettie said. "He smiled at me before he left and at the time I thought he was smiling at me because he knew I wasn't drinking. What if he was smiling because I was about to die?"

Beatrice shrugged. "Look at Tom's wine,"

Bettie presumed Tom was the black-eye man and Beatrice was right, Tom hadn't touched his wine so the poison hadn't come from there.

Bettie waved her hands in the air. "So I received an invitation two hours ago saying someone was going to die and they needed my help to stop it,"

"Great job you did," Beatrice said.

"Did any of you send the invitation?" Bettie asked.

The three people just looked at each other like none of them would dare do such a thing.

Bettie had to agree with them. If any of them had sent the invitation they would have known not to drink or eat or touch anything just in case poison was being used.

"So we have three problems to solve," Bettie said. "I need to know who sent me the invitation, what happened to your father and who tried to kill Tom here,"

Both Jasper, the man with the scar under the chin and Beatrice laughed.

"I'm sorry," Bettie said to the man with the scar. "What's your name?"

The man laughed. "Believe it or not, I'm the uncle of the family. Jeremiah Collins, the bum of the family who has apparently never accomplished anything in my life,"

Beatrice hissed and Bettie thought she was actually going to spit at him, there was definitely no love lost between them.

"How did you get your scar?" Bettie asked.

Bettie loved watching all the colour drain from Jeremiah's face.

"Um," he said. "I was cleaning snow off my drive two years ago and the shovel hit me,"

"We didn't have snow two years ago," Bettie

said.

"And you had that scar… three years ago but not before," Beatrice said.

"Fine," Jeremiah said trying to go for the hallway but the waiter appeared and blocked him. "I saw my brother that night he disappeared,"

"And you never said anything," Beatrice said trying to control her rage. Bettie took a few steps back just in case she lashed out.

"I was scared. I met my brother at the house that night and paid the waiter a thousand pounds the next day to say I wasn't,"

"And you still work here?" Bettie asked to the waiter.

The waiter smiled. "I love the family and I actually love the work,"

Bettie was surprised but the waiter seemed nice enough.

"I met my brother here after he found out about the affair because his wife had sent nudes to him instead of Jasper,"

Jasper looked as if he was about to die and really wanted the ground to swallow him up. Bettie loved hearing about people's secrets.

"I never wanted anything to happen but it simply turned into a massive argument. I said just divorce the woman but he didn't believe in divorce,"

"So you kept pressing daddy and he swung at you," Beatrice said as she rubbed her left arm.

"When did the argument happen? Before or after

he went out to get the wine?" Bettie asked.

"After and we never drunk the wine. He was saving it for the wife,"

Bettie was glad these people were revealing their secrets to her because at least the night of the 2nd December 2019 was starting to make sense.

Mr Collins travelled home after deployment to find his home empty and his wife said she was on her way back so he goes out to get a bottle of wine, then Collins received a series of nude photos of his wife that wasn't meant for him and he suddenly realises she was having an affair.

Yet Bettie couldn't understand another question now, what had happened to the wine?

"I need to speak to your mother," Bettie said to Beatrice with a lot more force than she intended to.

Beatrice looked at the ground. "You can't. She's... fragile. She isn't right in the head. And she... isn't a fan of Collins Day,"

"My boyfriend is a cop. One call from me and he will come running and he will investigate all of this including the assault from Jeremiah, the affair and everything else," Bettie said.

Beatrice stood up perfectly straight so Bettie knew there was more secrets to uncover but she believed that everyone was allowed to have at least secrets to themselves. Hell she certainly did.

"I took her to a home yesterday," Beatrice said. "She has advanced dementia for the past year and a half. She kept thinking that the waiter was my father and, nothing has been going well for her,"

Well that was another dead end for the case.

Bettie just looked at poor unconscious Tom and really hoped that when the ambulance and paramedics got here she could have them run a little test for her.

She needed to know exactly what poison had tried to kill Tom.

Yet Bettie was still no closer to knowing who had wanted her here tonight, who had tried to kill Tom and most importantly what had happened to Mr Collins.

***

Bettie's boyfriend Graham had to be the sexiest man alive and she seriously loved Senior Scientist Zoey Quill because she had agreed to go late into the lab tonight to run a few tests for Bettie, Bettie was definitely going to have to buy Zoey and her husband and her children a very special present for Christmas.

A few hours later, Bettie was sitting at the wooden table again with Beatrice, Jasper and Jeremiah with the air still smelling of fresh salmon, freshly roasted pecans and strong bitter coffee that the waiter had just bought out when her phone buzzed with the test results.

There was no way in hell that Bettie could even pronounce or read the name of the toxin used against Tom but thankfully (and because Zoey was so amazing) she had included a layman's version of the toxin.

"A very rare nerve agent was placed into the

salmon tonight," Bettie said. "And this particular nerve agent has to be programmed with the DNA of the victim before it activates,"

"So we're safe?" Jasper and Jeremiah asked at the same time.

Bettie nodded but was still a little surprised that Jeremiah was Beatrice's uncle yet she had been hissing, coughing and holding her stomach all night like she had been poisoned.

"What's wrong with your stomach?" Bettie asked knowing that she really needed to get answers now.

Beatrice looked past Bettie and weakly at the young waiter. Bettie didn't know whether to be concerned or not that it was fair to say the waiter had gotten Beatrice pregnant.

"That's why you stay as the waiter," Bettie said. That made a lot of sense but the nerve agent could only have come from one source that was possible for Bettie to understand.

The waiter went over, stood next to Beatrice and kissed her. And it was nice to see that they were in true love and not some fling that had ended in a pregnancy.

"Did your father ever bring back things from the Navy?" Bettie asked.

Beatrice held the waiter's hand so tight that her knuckles had turned white. "Yes, he bought back little things but he always kept them locked in a safe,"

Bettie just laughed because she finally realised what was going on, how someone had tried to kill

Tom and what had happened to Mr Collins three years ago.

Someone, not Mr Collins, was living in the walls.

"Have you ever heard sounds in the walls?" Bettie asked. "Have you ever heard sounds like someone was walking about at night?"

Beatrice's eyes widened. "My mother... she said someone pushed her down the stairs when she broke her leg I never believed her. I lied about when she broke her leg but she did break it four months before my father disappeared,"

"And my brother constantly moaned about food going missing," Jeremiah said. "Nothing weird has happened for years though. No food or anything,"

Bettie just nodded. "This old house has a lot of hollow spaces in-between the walls and I think if we open up some of these walls then we'll find something very disturbing,"

"You think... my daddy's inside?" Beatrice said.

Bettie took out her phone and called Graham. She didn't have the heart to agree with Beatrice but they did need a team of crime scene techs here immediately.

There was a lot of answers to find. No matter how disturbing they might be.

***

The constant low sounds of crime scene techs in their white uniforms, police sirens and Beatrice and the two remaining men giving statements filled the air as Bettie stood there outside in the icy cold winter night with her beautiful sexy Graham standing next to her.

Thankfully he was wearing a massive thick coat that Bettie clung to in case it would warm her up, Bettie was just glad that their little angels were asleep with Bettie's nephew Sean and his boyfriend harry watching over them. At least they were warm and toasty tonight.

Despite all the police cars and white crime scene vans outside, Bettie was still pleased that Beatrice's house looked beautiful and Christmassy outside as it had earlier with plenty of gravity-defying light displays in the shapes of angels, reindeer and snowmen. It was like you were about to walk into a winter wonderland.

And not a house filled with lies, deceit and secrets.

Graham's phone buzzed, took it out and gasped before showing the photo to Bettie. Bettie was amazed that the crime scene techs had found an entire network of narrow spaces in-between the old walls with remains of food wrappings, matches and water bottles littered throughout.

Yet the photo was of the perfectly mummified body of Mr Collins who was wrapped up tightly in a tarp and stuffed at the end of one of the passages that the person living inside the walls had made for themselves.

Bettie felt so disgusted because it was flat out wrong for someone to live inside the walls instead of living in their own house. The things this person could have seen was a horrific invasion of privacy but at least it explained a lot.

It explained why Beatrice's mother had said a man pushed her down the stairs, it explained why Mr Collins' brother didn't know what had happened to his brother after he left and what had happened to the wine, and it finally explained what happened to Mr Collins the night of the 2nd December 2019.

"What do you think happened that night?" Graham asked as he finished texting the crime scene techs because apparently the scene was far too busy, fragile and chaotic to risk Graham contaminating it.

"I think the man or woman came out the walls looking for food that night. He found Mr Collins angry and frustrated about his wife's affair and Mr Collins caught him or her. There was a fight and Mr Collins died," Bettie said.

"Then the killer took him into the walls to avoid anyone finding the body. But just imagine living with your own murder victim for so long?" Graham asked.

Bettie just laughed. "Babe, you realise what we do for a living. And you think a man living in the walls is the weirdest?"

"Fair point," Graham said, kissing her on the head.

"But where is the man or woman now?" Bettie asked. "And we know what happened to Mr Collins but what happened to Tom and who invited me?"

"Detective!" a uniformed officer standing by the

police tape shouted to Graham and then the officer gestured to a man engulfed in the shadow of the bright streetlamps.

Graham waved him through and Bettie instantly knew who this man was. He was the man living in the walls.

Bettie just stared at the very, almost dangerously thin man walk towards them, he was clean-shaved, in good health and looked rather handsome for a man in his late fifties.

The man was wearing black jogging bottoms, a very nice red t-shirt and a thick puffer jacket that suited him perfectly.

"Why kill him?" Bettie asked. Graham didn't seem to be following.

"I never meant to do that Miss English," the man said. "I was made homeless after my divorce and I had nothing but I was once a bricklayer and my father worked on this house,"

"So you knew about the gaps in the wall," Bettie said.

"Of course and my father was a cowboy builder. He didn't put in any insulation or anything so it was hardly a health hazard,"

"It's still illegal," Graham said.

Bettie waved him silent and gestured the man to continue.

"I knew the family always celebrated their silly little Collins Day tonight so I wanted... I wanted someone to finally discover the truth, because, he keeps talking to me,"

Bettie hugged the man for some reason she didn't understand but she could tell that he wasn't a bad person, he was just a man that had been forced by a situation to react.

Granted Bettie never would have decided to live in the walls of a house if she was homeless, but she could understand if someone was desperate enough.

"I never meant to kill Mr Collins but he caught me and I hate living with that corpse anyway. Please arrest me. At least you guys have heating, meals and free water. You have any idea how annoying it is having to wake up in the middle of the night just to get a day's supply of water,"

Bettie smiled and shook her head as Graham cuffed the man and arrested him for murder.

"Why did you try to kill Tom? You must have seen where Mr Collins kept the illegal things we bought back from the Navy and programmed the nerve agent," Bettie said.

The man's smile deepened. "I never wanted to kill Tom. I was aiming for Beatrice. I didn't know you needed to programme the nerve agent so that only means one thing, doesn't it Miss English?"

Bettie waved Graham so he took the man over to the nearest police car and Bettie was just shocked at yet another secret this family held. Mr Collins had programmed the nerve agent to kill Tom before he died, Bettie wasn't even sure she wanted to know why Mr Collins wanted to kill him (maybe he believed it was Tom who was having the affair with the wife) but Bettie knew one thing for sure.

She was really glad that the man, whoever he was, had invited her tonight so she could uncover the secrets, lies and deceptions that had been eating this family away for so long. And now, hopefully, just hopefully Beatrice could find some peace and move on from Collins Day.

And as Bettie went home to kiss her two little angels goodnight, she really hoped that was true. Because she had seen first-hand the sheer cost of people not being able to move on from the past.

It never ended well and it never led to a happy Christmas.

CHRISTMAS OBSESSION
4th December 2022
Rochester, England

Savannah Thomas absolutely loved the sheer amazement of the Christmas season with all its wonderful lights, foods and presents. She seriously couldn't have loved the Christmas season anymore. Savannah had already planned her December perfectly down to every single last breath-taking detail, she had already planned to see her parents, her sisters and her nephews.

This Christmas was just going to be amazing.

Savannah stood in front of her spectacular Christmas tree that her and her boyfriend Scott had cut down only last weekend. Savannah just flat out loved how the massive pine tree with its perfectly straight branches stretched all the way from her brown hard wooden oak floor (perfectly polished of course) until it just about touched her bright white ceiling.

The Christmas tree was stunningly beautiful with its bright red, blue and green LED lights that radiated pure holiday cheer and the little shiny, freshly polished bulbuls were just heavenly touches on the already amazing tree.

Savannah had loved Christmas ever since she was a little girl and she had always enjoyed singing, reading stories and opening presents by her parents' wonderfully warm coal fire. It was a shame that Savannah didn't have a fire of her own but that didn't matter because there were plenty of other great ways to spread Christmas cheer.

Her own parents and schoolfriends had questioned her all the time about why the hell she liked Christmas so much. especially as they thought it was strange that her Christmas obsession (such a strong and foul word) only increased with age.

But to Savannah those children and adults that lost their Christmas magic were just silly. Because surely Christmas got more and more magical with each passing year because adults could do so much more with their holidays.

Savannah always worked so much harder at Christmas just so she could buy more and more and more Christmas decorations. No one could ever have too many Christmas decorations, surely?

The breathtaking, delightful smell of rich buttery pastries cooking away in the oven along with sweet aromas of mince pies, Swiss rolls and rich boozy fruit cake filled the house. And Savannah seriously couldn't wait for the big day in a few weeks time.

This was going to be just a magical, sensational Christmas with her parents and boyfriend that she seriously hoped it was never going to end.

The sound of Christmas music playing in the background was so sweet, relaxing and Savannah just felt her soul was singing in sheer pleasure that she was surrounded by so much Christmas magic.

Someone thundered on her front door.

Savannah forced herself to take a deep breath of the pure Christmas-scented air. She really hoped whoever had banged on her front door hadn't damaged the precious Christmas wreath on the freshly red-painted wooden door.

That would be a crime against Christmas and all things good.

Savannah just shook her head and smiled as she went through her long tinsel-covered living room that sparkled in the glow of her living room lights, out through the hallway that had so many amazing Santa figures that Savannah couldn't see her hallway walls anyway then she went to the front door.

Her front door was thankfully covered in enough fake snow that she even tricked herself for a moment that the door handle was icy cold, but it wasn't. It was wonderful and toasty warm, just like how Christmas was meant to be.

Savannah opened the door and smiled out as the blinding, radiant light hit her as all her thousands upon thousands of Christmas lights shone out pure

Christmas magic onto the long urban road.

Then she instantly frowned when she saw a horrible group of three men wearing long dark trench coats.

Savannah instantly hated the sight of them. They were so disgusting and unchristmasy, they had to be criminals or something.

Savannah just looked at each of them. Each one of them were so foul, like the one on her left was definitely an elderly man with a stupid blue jumper underneath that made him certainly look his age. The man in the middle looked so young with his cute handsome face, short black hair and foul innocent looking eyes.

The man on the right was just awful with his fat belly, brown beard and balding head. He was like some perversion of Christmas that Savannah just wanted to kill.

But she forced herself to take a deep breath of the wonderfully icy cold Christmas air, and she smiled at each other of them.

"Young Miss," the man with the belly said. "Would you like to change your life for the better?"

"That is nothing better than Christmas," Savannah said sharply.

"But Christmas is fake. Christmas is unholy. God does not like Christmas," the blue jumper man said.

Savannah wanted nothing more than to kill these people exactly where they stood. All Savannah wanted was to enjoy her Christmas with her boyfriend and family and these stupid people wanted to stop her. The nerve of these mortal fools was incredible.

"Christ is not real but God is. Accept God and Christianity into your heart and be reborn anew," the handsome man said.

Savannah spat at their feet. "Christmas is whatever I make it. Christmas brings me joy. That is all that matters,"

The three men laughed.

"How do you dare celebrate the creation and a holiday dedicated to a being that does not exist. God will never forgive you. Let me help you on the road to forgiveness," the handsome man said.

Savannah just looked at the handsome man. He really was rather attractive in a way, and maybe if she placed him next to her boyfriend then the three of them could have some fun but he hated Christmas so it could never ever work out.

That was a damn shame because he was actually rather hot and Savannah would have loved to know what sort of body the handsome man had under that black trench coat.

The man with the belly grabbed her wrist. Tight.

"Repent. Daughter of Christ. Daughter of False Prophets. Daughter that is an enemy of God," he said.

Savannah had met extremists before and she had plenty of Jewish friends but these people weren't Jews. Jews were great people, very nice and very kind. Savannah just hated that these Christ-haters couldn't accept that other people wanted to celebrate his holiday.

Savannah ripped her hand away and just knew that she needed to deal with these men once and for all so she did.

Savannah bowed her head slightly and for some reason she just knew that she needed to invite them inside.

"Please my saviours," Savannah said. "Come into my corrupted home, murdered home and please guide me to the Light without Christmas,"

Savannah hated saying the foul twisted words that betrayed every single thing she believed in but she had to say that. She had to protect her Christmas one way or another.

The three stupid men nodded their thanks and Savannah led them through the hallway and living room and she absolutely loved listening to their gasps of horror, and then Savannah led them out to the kitchen area.

Savannah had freshly decorated her kitchen and she was still getting used to the sensational silver chrome cabinets, worktops and oven that shined so brightly at Christmas as the various lights she had scattered around was reflected perfectly off the chrome.

Then the three men screamed in utter terror as they saw Savannah's marvellous dining table. Savannah really loved that her boyfriend had bought her a massive wooden farm table a few weeks back for their new kitchen.

And it was even better that he, Savannah's parents and now the three stupid men were going to be able to spend forever around the table as their bodies slowly rotted together.

Savannah had even wrapped some tinsel around the sliced throats of her boyfriend and parents to make them love Christmas as much as she did. If only they didn't try to send her away over Christmas to some mental hospital then maybe they would still be alive.

Savannah would never ever miss her precious Christmas for anyone.

Thankfully Savannah's boyfriend was still holding the large freshly polished carving knife that she had killed him with, cleaned and then placed back in his hand for keeping.

So she picked it up and went over to the three stupid anti-Christmas men that were frozen in utter terror.

***

25th December 2022

Unknown Location, England

When Christmas day came around, Savannah absolutely loved the delightful scents of lemons, oranges and bleach that filled the air. It was just a wonderful smell that made the sensational taste of Christmas cake, mulled wine and breath-taking gingerbread form on her tongue.

Savannah had been at the mental hospital for

about a week now and Savannah just loved it. She loved her little bright white cell with only a small bed to keep her company and the floor and temperature might have been cold and anti-Christmas but that was fine.

Because Savannah never wanted to live inside her cell at the mental hospital, that wasn't right, positive or Christmassy. All that Savannah wanted to do was simply live in her mind, her memories and relive her memories of Christmas over and over and over again each second of every single day.

She wanted to relive her memories of tinsel, food and presents every single second, and most importantly she wanted to relive the moments of killing her boyfriend, parents and the three foul men as much as she could. Their blood was thick and dark and red just like her precious tinsel.

A bright white door opened inside Savannah's cell and she smiled at the man wearing thick black glasses, a white lab coat and carrying a clipboard.

"Merry Christmas doctor," Savannah said smiling. Oh she hoped he was having a good Christmas and she wasn't a burden.

"The detectives found a ton of bodies in your garden. You know? The bodies hanging off your large pine tree and painted bright red and green and blue. Do you know what I'm talking about?"

Savannah just grinned because she really did. She often didn't go into the garden at Christmas because it just didn't feel Christmassy at all for her, but this year she wanted to do something special so she had.

Savannah had killed her neighbours, wrapped them up in plastic wrapping into balls and she had painted them before she had hung them from trees in her garden. That really did bring the wonderful garden to life.

"You're going to spend a very long time in here Miss Thomas," the doctor said. "Merry Christmas and I'll see you in the new year,"

Savannah just laughed to herself because she really was having a wonderful merry Christmas and she really wouldn't want her life any other way.

Because any other way simply wouldn't be as Christmassy as her way.

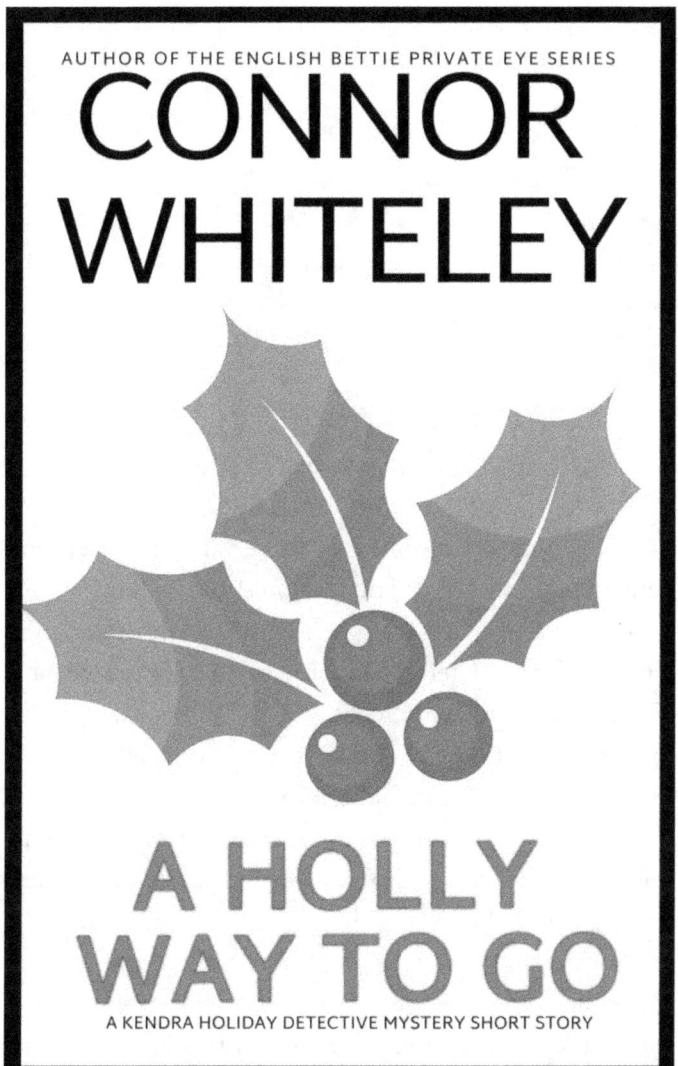

A HOLLY WAY TO GO
14th December 2022
London, England

Normally on a cold December afternoon, retired detective Kendra O'Connor would be thinking about what to cook her and her amazing husband for dinner, planning her grand Christmas celebrations and deciding what to wear to one of the Christmas parties that she went to every single year without fail.

This wasn't a normal afternoon.

Kendra stood in a very dense forest filled with thick twisted pine, oak and silver birch trees with their leafless branches stretching out in all sorts of directions. Kendra was standing right next to one silver birch that had two branches so intertwined that she just knew that whatever caused those branches to become so twisted couldn't have been short of brutal.

Kendra much preferred the wonderful coolness of the ground and she was more than that the morning frost, mist and fog had mostly been burnt around by the weak dim sun that Kendra sadly knew would set in the next hour. And then the temperature would seriously drop.

Kendra was already wearing her thickest winter coat, gloves and trousers that she owned. She was a 67-year-old for goodness sake, she was fairly sure that she wasn't even meant to be out in these close-to-freezing temperatures.

But as the hints of roasted peanuts, nutmeg cookies and sawdust filled the air, Kendra was glad she was here in the icy cold forest without a shred of warmth because she was here on a very dark and twisted and awful case that Kendra just wanted to solve.

Kendra's best friends retired police officer Patricia Nelson, wearing a long black fake-fur coat, hiking boots and pink gloves, stood to her left and it was surprising to see Patricia without her black laptop bag. She was the techie one of the group and Kendra was always amazed at how the 70-year-old woman was good on the laptop. She could probably outdo Kendra's grandchildren with her computer skills.

Then to Kendra's right was her other friend and the point of contact with the Police Commissioner, was Retired Detective Jeff Long. Kendra had to admit that the atmosphere was a little tense between Jeff and Patricia because poor Jeff (bless him) had been working around Kendra's kitchen table and Patricia had placed her laptop on her seat because the table was covered in folders.

Then silly Jeff had thought the laptop was a very thin cushion so he sat on it, cracked the outer casing so Patricia was a little fuming with him at the moment.

Kendra just hoped her anger might warm up the air around them.

And they were all here today because they were members of the cold case task force that always sought to solve London's weirdest, toughest and more brutal cold cases.

And this one was particularly new.

The three of them had spent the morning trying to solve the disappearance and most probably murder of a 26-year-old male university student called George Carrie. He studied biomedical Science at University College London, was liked by everyone and had a great boyfriend that loved him dearly.

George had disappeared five years ago after going out on a night out with some university friends, and the boyfriend was busy studying for his exams in the library with over 100 witnesses, the family was up North and wasn't in London for the disappearance and not a single one of the friends or people at the university had a motive to kidnap George.

There were no leads. Not a shred of evidence and the only reason the police believed George was missing in the first place was because of a single frame of security camera footage showing George running and checking behind him as he presumably ran away from something or someone.

"Do you think we'll find him?" Patricia asked as she blew into her gloves.

Kendra slowly nodded as the three of them focused right ahead of them on the two teams of white-clothed crime scenes techs that were currently carefully slicing, cutting and hacking their way through a massive pile of Holly in an effort to get to a festive tarp that was hidden under it all.

"I just don't understand how a killer got the body out here in the first place," Jeff said.

The three of them had only got the case this morning and because of the sheer coldness of the temperature and Kendra's husband working, they had agreed to work in Kendra's kitchen. Which Kendra was more than happy with because it meant her coffee machine, cake and ice cream in the kitchen were very close to hand.

Kendra still didn't exactly know how she was going to explain to her husband later on that each of them had done a large tub of ice cream, three mugs of coffee and finished off a large Victoria sponge between them all.

They had all done their fair share of serious eating today and Kendra supposed that was why it was good to come into the icy cold forest today to see the discovery of the body.

If the body was here at all.

Kendra had to admit the case hadn't been easy at all because the three of them had to somehow work out what George was running away from, but thankfully because everyone was on social media these days and Patricia had the ethically questionable computer skills to run an advanced social media search, Patricia managed to find something.

After a few moments, Patricia had managed to find thirty images of George running away from a group of UCL students from another course and they were really shouting and pointing at George like he was a monster.

So Kendra had phoned up the university to see if they had any records of the students and they said they didn't. But Kendra just knew they were lying so she called up one of her friends at the admin office and she got her to give her the names of students.

Jeff had then seriously failed to conduct a basic social media search of the five students, which Kendra and Patricia had laughed about. Thankfully Patricia managed to find out that the five students were all still friends, going to the university and they were all passionate hikers.

Kendra didn't know if that made them crazy or not, there was nothing worse to Kendra than wanting to walk endlessly around. She would have preferred to dance, run or do something that would at least keep her warm.

Then that's the exact moment when Jeff had made himself another mug of coffee, Patricia had placed her laptop on the seat and Jeff had sat on it. Even now the massive crack echoed in Kendra's ears.

"I still couldn't believe that chunky thing still

worked," Patricia said grinning.

Kendra playfully hit her best friend, because Kendra had jokingly said when the laptop had broken that Patricia should use Kendra's computer that she got in the 80s. She was amazed that it still worked but it was a massive chunky white thing, so it can had taken about 30 minutes to move from upstairs to the kitchen and that's when Kendra had a great idea.

Clearly the entire case revolved around the fact that George had been running from the students and they had managed to work out that he was probably making his way towards the university library, hopefully so his boyfriend could protect him.

But Kendra couldn't understand why George had ran past police stations, police officers on patrol and even a security campus hub.

Why not go there for help?

So Kendra had searched medical records for the boyfriend and Jeff had managed to find a bank account charge to the boyfriend for two weeks after the disappearance to a private medical centre in the heart of London.

And Kendra, putting on her best posh person voice, pretended to be someone from the Department of Health's investigator division (the poor receptionist woman didn't even know that division wasn't real) and Kendra found out that the boyfriend had visited the medical centre with a small stab wound, and the private medical centre agreed not to inform the police on the patient's "obsessive demands".

Kendra had had no clue why the boyfriend had gotten stabbed and refused to tell the police about it, but the fact that George had done the same had to be connected.

Well, Kendra still couldn't believe that Jeff had killed off that theory in a second because he found newspaper reports about George when he was ten years old after his brother (who was also gay) was murdered by police officers in a homophobic attack, so it was little wonder why George didn't want to go to the police. He was probably more scared about being killed by them than the students chasing him.

Yet Kendra was so glad when Patricia had pinged the phones of the five students (legally of course) on the night of the disappearance and the three nights afterwards and that's when the case got so strange that it was all up to Kendra to figure it out.

"It was always the Holly," Kendra said to her best friends as an icy cold breeze brushed past them and even the white-clothed crime scene techs seemed to shake for a moment.

"It was silly for the five students to come to the woods for the three nights after the murder hun," Patricia said.

"Yes," Kendra said, "but if they hadn't then they would be stuck with a body,"

Her best friends simply nodded as they watched the crime scene techs cut away the last of the holly bushes that covered some tarp underneath.

Once Kendra had gotten Patricia to ping the phones of the students, everyone had struggled to figure out how to find out what the students were doing. This particular forest was a well-known sex spot for students, drug den for dealers and robbery for the odd wealthy person who drove through here.

Patricia had tried to access the wildlife cameras in the forest but they didn't show the students whatsoever, but they did show plenty of other questionable activity.

Jeff had tried to get social media pictures and any pictures on the "interweb" as he sadly called it, but that failed to find the students in the woods.

So Kendra had figured out that Patricia needed to check the bank accounts of the five students and when that failed, they needed to check the parents' accounts.

That's when the truth was revealed because the mother of one of the five students bought twenty small holly bushes, a tarp and five shovels two days after the disappearance. So presumably the first night after the disappearance the students were looking for a spot to dump the body, the second night they perhaps started digging but they realised they didn't have the tools. Then the third night they got rid of the body.

"Detectives!" a crime scene tech shouted.

Kendra rushed over to them to the thick forest and just shook her head.

Patricia and Jeff gasped behind Kendra as all

three of them looked down at the opened tarp covering George's rotten body, but even with all the decay Kendra could still see all the marks, slashes and cuts in the tarp from the Holly.

"They covered him in Holly when he was still alive," Kendra said.

"And detectives, I ain't a scientist but I bet this needle contains drugs," one of the techs said.

Kendra just nodded as the tech placed the needle in an evidence bag. "The students drugged him to make sure he couldn't escape but they still wanted him to move about,"

"So he sliced himself on the thorns of Holly hun," Patricia said. "They always wanted him to suffer,"

"Jesus," Jeff said. "I'll call in the active detectives to take over,"

Kendra just nodded as she couldn't tear her eyes away from the rotten corpse at her feet. George must have been in so much pain, agony and torment as he died.

At least the five students were going to finally get what was coming to them.

And George could finally rest in peace.

***

Six hours later, Kendra, Patricia and Jeff sat round Kendra's large black marble coffee table in her living room with massive white mugs of hot chocolate and a very small plate with the remains of cheese sandwiches on them because after all the ice cream and cake from earlier, none of them wanted too much for their dinner.

Kendra was sure that her doctor was going to shout at her but she didn't care. It was almost Christmas and she would go back to her diet and healthy living in January like she always did.

Her living lights were on low and Kendra loved it like that because the lighting always helped to create such a festive atmosphere with the flashing rainbow colours of the Christmas lights on her tree as well.

Jeff had gotten the call just a moment ago from the active detectives and he had taken it in the kitchen so Kendra was really looking forward to knowing what was the result of the past six hours.

"All five students confessed," Jeff said. "They said that George's boyfriend had wanted to earn a little extra money before the Christmas period so he could buy his parents, siblings and boyfriend something extra nice. So he took the five students extra tutoring in their free time,"

Kendra was really starting to like the boyfriend more and more, it really did seem like he was a great person.

"Then one day when the boyfriend was round the students' dorm he discovered their drug operation because the students wanted to get him hooked on coke. The boyfriend said no and George told him not to do the tutoring anymore,"

"The student didn't like that hun, did they?"

"No Patty," Jeff said. "The students knew it was

only a matter of time before the boyfriend and George spoke up because they were against drugs. So the five students wanted to scare the boyfriend by kidnapping George,"

Kendra leant forward. She really wasn't liking where this was going.

"The students grabbed George, knocked him out and put him in a van. Then George got free and the students knocked him again,"

Kendra waved her hands in the air. "Okay but how do five university students get from knocking a man out to paralysing him with drugs and allowing him to die from exposure whilst Holly bushes grow around him?"

Jeff bit his lip. "One of the students had a girlfriend doing a biomedical course, she's been arrested because she came up with the plan to get rid of George's body,"

Kendra just shook her head as the three of them sat in perfect silence. This really was such a weird case because poor George and his boyfriend had done nothing wrong and they had still died.

It was a terrible tale so close to the big day itself, and George would never be able to celebrate another Christmas with the man he loved, and his family would never be able to see the delight on his face when he opened his presents.

Even now Kendra loved seeing that with her own children.

Kendra was more than glad those six students

were going to spend the rest of their lives in prison. Because that was exactly what they deserved.

And as Kendra went to grab the front door because her amazing sexy husband was home, Kendra just knew she wasn't having any holly in the house for ages just in case it grew over her and she suffered the same scary fate as George Carrie.

MYSTERIOUS CHRISTMAS

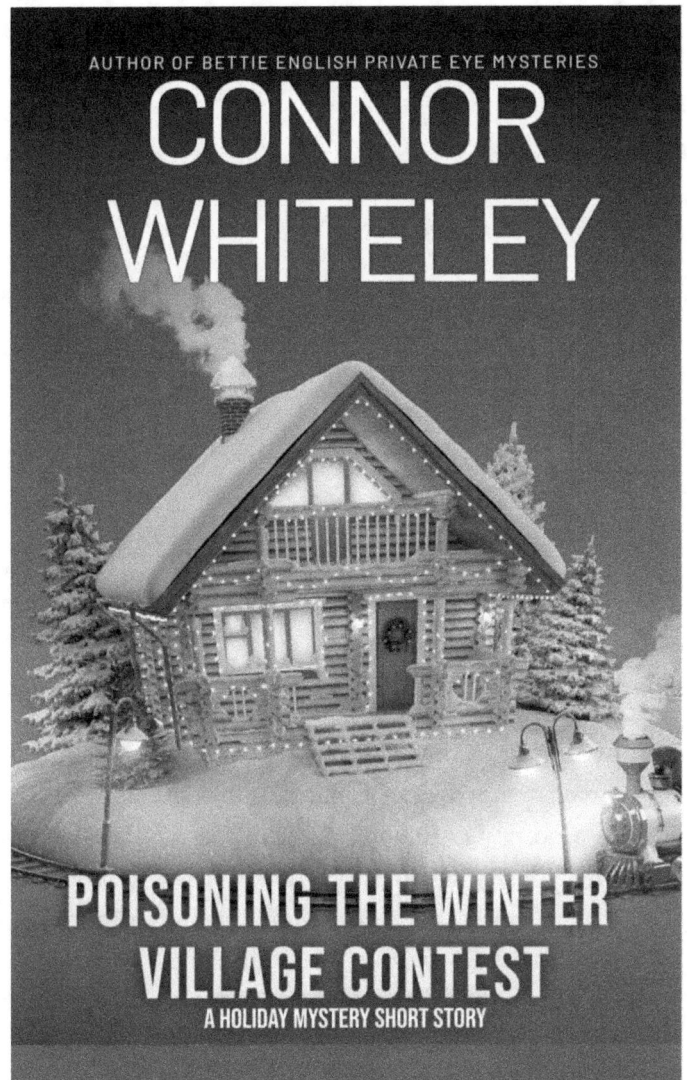

POISONING THE WINTER VILLAGE CONTEST

19th December 2022

Southeast England

Now I fully believe that the vast majority of small villages, towns and even cities have some sort of flat out weird contest for the holiday season. I once lived in a village that had a "Best Peppermint Cream" contest and that was a particularly great year because I do love all things peppermint, but there are some holiday traditions. Including "The Best Killer Santa Costume" that was probably the weirdest I've come across but I'm sure there are plenty more out there.

And you see before I continue any further I actually need you to understand weird this village is that I live in, and just how crazy how of the traditions are so you can understand that what I ended up doing was relatively sane compared to the contests.

You see my name is Jo-Jo O'Dell and I seriously love the holidays, Christmas trees and anything to do with peppermint. And up until three days ago I worked as the Chief Operations Manager for the county's sanitation network.

I loved my job because I was so good at it. I completely updated their prehistoric computer systems, I made the sanitation network more effective and cheaper to run and I was beloved by everyone.

Well, that's what I thought.

But it turns out in very conservative rural Southeast England, people don't like it when a gay man comes into the village with his husband, Patrick, over twenty years and two beautiful children, gets the top job at the only real employment centre in the area and manages to outdo everyone.

So apparently, there was a complaint made against me, because *apparently* I was being a bad worker, my bosses refused to support me and well, I got the sack for nothing that I did and the initial complaints were all lies anyway.

Tonight I would thankfully get my revenge though.

I was standing with my amazing hunk of a husband who was easily a foot taller than me with massive muscles, an insanely hot body and a slight blond beard that I have to admit I did like playing with at night.

Our two wonderful children were having a sleepover with their best friends tonight, and they were 17-year-olds anyway, so we were standing in the massive town hall structure that was very impressive for a small town/ village. I really liked its large white marble pillars with gold veining that helped to add such depth and texture to the large square hall.

The walls were freshly painted cream, the ceiling was a little patching but poor Jim had to do the painting and he was unfortunately half-blind so I'm amazed he managed this much. I just wished he took the money I offered him to go and get the surgery to fix his sight.

He refused and spat at my feet.

The entire hall was covered in beautiful Christmas decorations with massive banters, streams of tinsel and child-made paper chains in a rainbow of colours hung from everywhere. And the sweet aromas of wonderful peppermint, ginger and mulled wine filled the air making the sensational taste of Christmas cake form on my tongue.

"Evening Jo-Jo," an elderly woman said as she walked past me.

I smiled at her because Mrs Oliver was a great woman, she was kind, helpful and seriously hadn't cared when she caught me and Patrick making out in the closet of the town hall. And amazingly enough that actually kicked off a friendship with the elderly lady for twenty years.

Amazing how things worked out.

"Is everything set up for tonight?" Patrick asked me with a devilish grin.

I simply nodded because it was only two hours ago that Patrick had told me he had also been fired from working in the local council because of lies, deceit and corruption so I told him my plan and he wanted to help.

Of course by this point there was nothing to help with but I told him to enjoy the sight.

Because the thing about two gay men that met each other when we were both homeless, hungry and very angry at our parents for kicking us out because we were gay, was that we were rather cruel to people that we didn't like. Just like how the world was cruel to us for no reason whatsoever.

As soon as I was fired I used my sanitation knowledge and put it to good use because the interesting thing about sanitation networks is they are very, very prone to breaking. Especially when a certain person, also known as me, knows exactly what values to shut off and my bosses at the local council never ever thought to actually lock me out of the system.

Well, even if they had it wouldn't have saved them because I had used over twenty different backdoors for myself so I could get into the computer system whenever I wanted. And wow, have I been busy over the past few days and now everything was going to show up.

And things were going to get very interesting, very quickly because the water tank in the town hall that supplied the building with drinking water was currently being flooded with wee-water.

"Places everyone!" a young and rather hot man

shouted.

I had never really liked the Deputy Major too much because he wasn't exactly friendly towards my kids, my house and Mrs Oliver so I was looking forward to teaching him a lesson on tonight of all nights.

Because tonight was The Village Winter Contest which involved two things, both were things that I highly approved of and normally entered myself. The first part of the contest was who could make the best peppermint drink in the entire village and the second part was who could make the best miniature village.

All around us there were massive wooden tables with young and older, fat and slim and hip and seriously not people standing behind them with large mugs on the tables.

It was so amazing to smell all the different cocktails, mocktails and soft drinks get mixed together to create the best peppermint drink ever. The hall was filled with delightful sounds of banging, stirring and panicked voices scared about getting something wrong.

It was all rubbish of course because the so-called prize money a person was meant to get never arrived in their bank account. There were plenty of theories over the years why but I knew that it went into the Mayor's bank account and no one seemed to care.

Almost no one.

That was one of the advantages of having a husband that worked with computers, had a Masters degree in computer science and basically had no problem breaking laws to help people. I really did love that man so we *might* have hacked the Mayor's bank account and now all the winners from the past twenty years had their prize money, with interest of course.

"What about the water?" my beautiful husband asked me.

I laughed. "Just relax babe,"

Now he did have a good point in all fairness because I was now quickly realising that barely anyone here tonight was using water in their special drinks. Which I supposed was because I might have also added a little, chemical substance that would give whoever drank the water horrific diaherria.

And before you think about it, no this couldn't hurt anyone because I had already set off an alarm and prescheduled a warning message to be sent out at a certain time. Meaning the problem should be detected after the judges drink the water but before anyone else does.

I'm sure some of you might be wondering what I have against the four judges tonight, but let me tell you I have every single damn right to poison these people. The first and dickhead judge was the Mayor himself, the second was the Deputy Mayor and the third was the local history teacher.

Now I actively encourage people to learn outside the things that school teaches you because school is rather limited in the grand scheme of things and I understand why. There's only so much you can learn in the school day.

But when the local teacher, a local woman called Elizabeth, decided to cover LGBT+ History, I was interested because I didn't know that much myself. But to point to my kids in the middle of the history lesson and talk *about* them like they weren't in the room, they weren't real people and they were mere examples of equalities, that was pushing her luck I thought.

It was even worse when she concluded her mini-lecture by commenting on how *the kids turned out well considering the sheer lack of femineity and masculinity in their lives.* Well even now I have no idea what I would say to her but at least my daughter and son had some... choice words for the teacher.

I do love my family.

And the fourth final judge bless him, was a Old Doc George, the local doctor who was really trying to force me and my husband to be sterilized so we didn't spread our gay DNA to anyone else.

Need I say more?

"Can the first contestant come up?" the old fat mayor said as he sat down at the wooden table on the far end of the town hall.

My beautiful husband grinned on as a little middle-aged man bought up a tray containing four large glasses of piping hot peppermint hot chocolate and this man certainly would have used water from the town hall.

All four judges gulped down the drink, had a massive overdramatic gasp and quietly wrote notes about the drink in their little black notebooks.

"Next," the Mayor said.

I was a little confused as to why my wee-water plan wasn't working immediately but I was a patient man.

Next a very tall elegant lady wearing a long sweeping white dress walked past us holding a very large trap filled with a peppermint malt drink. Again she would have used the water from the town hall.

The judges smiled, gulped down their drink and gasped again. They laughed at each other because they had a malt moustache under their noses and they made their silly little notes.

"I thought-"

I kissed my husband on the lips to shut him up because I really couldn't understand why the plan wasn't working.

"Third one," the mayor said but I noticed something was wrong with his voice. It sounded strained.

A very young teenage girl went over to the judges with three shot glasses filled with her clean liquid.

The whole cycle continued again but after the judges wrote down the notes in their notebooks they started frowning at each other.

They all farted again and again until they didn't.

Then things got very, very messy for everyone. And things got very, very funny for the two of us.

***

I think the most amazing thing about poisoning people without anyone knowing that you've actually done it is very simple. It is that when shit hits the fan rather literally and all the sanitation warning systems go off, everyone turns to you, you get your old job back with tenure and double the salary in exchange for "helping" them get rid of the problem.

So after the chocolate fountains started and everyone got the emergency warning about the sanitation system failing all over the county, the mayor rushed over to me and begged me to help him.

I did in exchange for the double the pay and tenure position, so now I really couldn't get sacked now forever.

In all fairness it had only taken me two hours to fix my problem but a good hour of that was me just deleting any evidence that I had contaminated the system, and for good measure I played on my phone for another two hours so I made it look like it was an impossible job that only I could do.

And it worked and all without a single innocent person getting ill too. That was perfect.

No one saw the judges for the next two weeks, no one won this year's Village Winter Contest but at least the prize money somehow ended up in all the contestant's bank accounts, even the ones I didn't like, and even some charities benefited.

That husband of mine, if it was actually him of course, was a great man that I seriously loved more than anything in the world.

And with my revenge done, my job returned to me and now I had twice as much money, I really was looking forward to Christmas because it seriously was a magical time of year where literally anything could happen.

Now if you don't mind as I mentioned earlier, my two children are staying at their friend's for the night so me and my husband have some alone time.

And believe me, we definitely plan to make good, wholesome use of it.

MYSTERIOUS CHRISTMAS

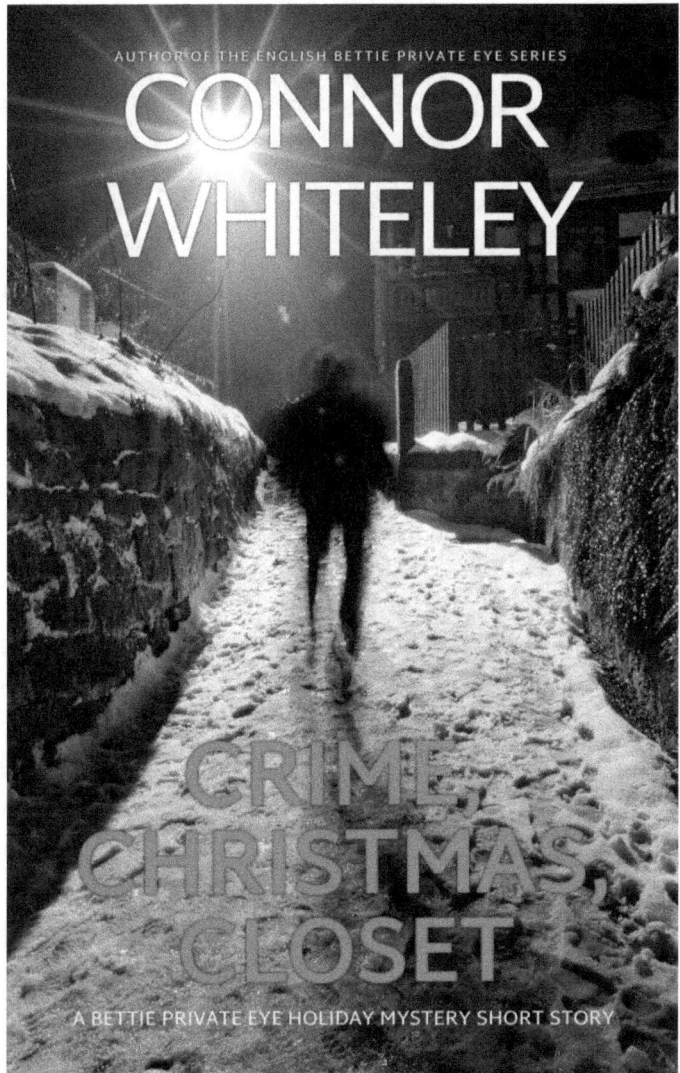

CRIME, CHRISTMAS, CLOSET

Bettie English, Private Eye, opened her eyes only to realise, she couldn't see. She even strained her eyes forcing them to open as wide as she possibly could. It didn't matter. She could only see darkness.

As she tried to move, Bettie felt something cover her skin, hold her tight and constrict her movements. She wasn't going anywhere anytime soon.

Knowing she was trapped for a moment, or the foreseeable future (she didn't know), Bettie pressed her back against the smooth cold surface of something. For a moment Bettie wondered if it was even worth trying to guess where she was, but that's when she felt something.

She hissed a little as a headache corkscrewed across her head and sent a wave of pain over her. Bettie kept hissing for a few seconds before the headache passed and Bettie knew something bad had happened.

Breathing in the musty air of wherever she was, Bettie tried to focus on what she remembered. She couldn't. She felt as if there was something she was meant to remember, but she couldn't. The smell of mustard started to chip away at her concentration, it was so strong, so ugly, so awful.

But Bettie smiled because even that was a clue of sorts, lots of objects and places and perfumes didn't smell musty so she just needed to figure what places did smell musty.

Trying to ignore the awful smell, Bettie focused on everything else, but she was really focusing on sound. If she could hear something, music, cars, whatever. Then she might be able to figure out where she was.

After a few moments of listening, Bettie heard some Christmas songs, some children playing in the snow (maybe) in the distance and something else. Someone opening, searching and banging cupboards nearby.

Bettie was sure they were all the clues she needed to figure out what was going on, but she hissed a little more as the headache returned for a few moments.

Taking a few deep breaths of the musty air, she tried to stretch her fingers in case she could feel something on the walls or maybe even a door or light switch. But her fingers were covered in something too.

In some attempt to find out what she was covered in, Bettie rubbed her fingers as much as she could (which wasn't a lot) against the material and Bettie frowned. She was sure she had concussion but Bettie swore she was feeling tinsel or something.

Bettie shook her head at the stupidity of her being tied up with Christmas decorations and tinsel no less, but as a private eye she couldn't say she hadn't seen weird things.

Pressing her head against the smooth cold wall

(?), Bettie focused on remembering what had happened. She was a private eye so she had to be here for a case, she just couldn't remember what case. It could be civil, kidnapping or theft for all Bettie knew.

But a fragment of a memory reminded her about something. It was new and Bettie hadn't done very many of these cases but she had recently got her bounty hunter license.

At first Bettie hadn't wanted to get it because no one uses bounty hunters in the UK but Bettie always liked a challenge.

But Bettie still felt as if there was something she was meant to remember. Something about what happened. Something... she just didn't know but it felt important.

She cocked her head and felt something tinsel-like brush against her cheek as she wondered if she was here as a bounty hunter.

Bettie had no idea, it was possible. Her boyfriend Graham had suggested a few targets for her but she hadn't listened, she was too focused on... relationship things whenever she spoke about it. She still wasn't sure if she wanted children like he did.

The sound of opening, searching and banging cupboards nearby stopped and now it sounded like someone was walking up some stairs.

Then it hit Bettie and she felt some sweat drip down her back, neck and hands as it dawned on her she was in a closet. It made sense to Bettie and there were worse places to be tied up, she knew all about that from the time she was tied up in a car and driven around London.

But this was something else.

With sweat continuing to roll down her back,

neck and hands, Bettie needed to think about what to do. If there was a dangerous bounty target walking up the stairs to finish her off, she had to be ready.

She wished there was some light for her to see, maybe she would have been able to see something sharp or something thing to break her tinsel prison with. Yet there was still no light.

Pushing herself up, Bettie pushed her weight forward, fell and landed on something soft. She was glad it wasn't something hard.

Using her head, lips and cheeks, Bettie managed to rather impressively (if she did say so herself) feel that it was probably some kind of mattress that someone had stuffed into the closet.

Bettie swore under her breath as she really wanted something to help break free, she didn't want to be tied up, constricted or someone's prisoner. She had to be free and she had to solve the mystery of what happened to her.

A part of her wondered if she had been gone long enough for Graham to come back from home, notice she was gone and start searching for her. But Bettie remembered he was working late tonight because of an operation with the French.

The idea of her being gone for days briefly went through her mind but she quickly dismissed it. Partly out of utter terror that it was true and her friends and family couldn't find her, but she knew her family loved her too much to let her stay missing for so long. Especially her nephew.

Rolling over on the mattress, Bettie almost gagged as a massive whiff of mustard was kicked into the air.

The lights turned on.

Bettie blinked rapidly as her eyes adjusted to the bright light bulb hanging from the ceiling.

Looking up, Bettie's eyes narrowed on the little rectangular closet she was tied up in. She swore again as she felt her blood boil at herself for letting some criminal get the better of her.

Bettie looked at the white walls, door and mattress in the closet and wondered why someone wouldn't put more in here. It was almost like someone had either emptied it or made it just to trap her.

Her mind quickly started to come up with silly ideas about her being trapped by a serial killer, a trafficker or a kidnapper. But Bettie realised there was a much more pressing question.

Why did the lights turn on?

Bettie looked at herself and nodded as she saw she was tied up with blue, red and green tinsel that she hated. As much as Bettie loved Christmas she didn't like green tinsel, it wasn't an attractive colour and as for when her boyfriend got dressed up for Christmas, Bettie made sure he didn't wear green.

The sound of Christmas songs, children playing in the snow in the distance and someone walking right outside the closet made Bettie smile and her eyes narrow.

She knew normal people would be scared in this moment, but Bettie wasn't. She was excited, thrilled, ready for action. She wanted, needed to confront this criminal who dared trap her. Her plan was simple. Scream to scare the criminal.

The door opened.

Bettie screamed.

Someone else screamed.

Jumping back.

Bettie wormed out of the closet.

Climbing onto the other person.

She headbutted them.

Then she realised it was her nephew Sean. Bettie instantly recognised him from his black designer jeans, smooth face and long white coat.

As she stared wide-eyed at her nephew, she felt her stomach tighten and her spirit drop as she had just attacked her nephew. Her sister was going to shout at her that was for sure and as for his boyfriend Harry, Bettie didn't even want to think about that.

"Aunty want to get off me?" Sean said.

Bettie rolled off him as she heard Sean get some scissors and cut her free.

"What were you doing in a closet?" Sean asked smiling.

"I thought I would try it. You know what being in a closet is like," Bettie said.

Sean playfully hit her head.

"Seriously Aunty. Mum's been worried sick," Sean said as he finished cutting.

Bettie smiled as she stretched and felt joints, muscles and bones pop as they moved for the first time in hours.

"I don't know. Someone hit me from behind,"

"You don't remember do you Aunty?"

Bettie's eyebrows rose. "What?"

"You got Harry to run a background check on a cop friend of Graham's. He sent you the results and we didn't hear anything of you,"

"What's the time?"

"Six,"

Bettie nodded as her memory started to return to

her and remembered it all. She met Detective Inspector Lawrence two days ago at some awards ceremony. The food was nasty, cheap and awful so Bettie didn't taste too much and Graham avoided it all.

But when she met Lawrence there was something about him, the way he spoke, moved and acted. It was strange and then there was a rumour that Graham had mentioned in passing about him taking brides for politicians.

At first Bettie knew she was being paranoid but there weren't any cases that she was working on so she had the time. A quick internet search alone revealed a lot of good information about Lawrence. Lots of accusations, some evidence, no charges.

Returning her attention back to Sean, Bettie's eyes narrowed.

"How did you find me? And who was banging the cupboards?"

Sean looked to the floor. "I know you're with a cop, but you won't tell would you?"

Bettie smiled and shook her head. She didn't really want to hear his next sentence.

"Me and Harry pinged your phone,"

A part of Bettie wanted to chastise him for doing something so illegal but she could hardly talk these days. Bettie just hoped her sister wouldn't find out, she would burn Bettie alive for corrupting her son.

"The cupboards?" Bettie pressed.

"What about the cupboards?"

Bettie's eyes narrowed. "Before you found me. I heard someone opening, searching and banging cupboards. Was that you?"

Sean shook his head and they both smiled. If that

was the criminal then they had just made a very stupid mistake. There were plenty of cameras round the house, so Bettie and Sean rushed out and went to find their criminal.

***

Sitting on the cold brick wall outside the house she had just been trapped in, Bettie looked up and down the snowy road that looked rather magical with the white snow against the black sky, as she wondered who had kidnapped her. It made sense for it to be Lawrence but she needed proof.

As Bettie felt the cold wintery wind blow gently past as Bettie focused on all the semi-detached houses with their large drives and neatly arranged front gardens that were all covered in snow.

Whilst she was waiting for Sean to come back with his laptop, Bettie just sat there listening to the Christmas songs from inside the houses, children playing and the distant sounds of cars driving.

Returning to a thought from earlier, Bettie wondered if she was ever going to have children (she really didn't have anything else to think about), she loved Christmas with all the food, presents and family, but she wasn't sure if she wanted her own little family. Graham had spoken about it but she wasn't sure. She loved her job, she was a private eye through and through, and Bettie had seen the terrible things humans could do.

So the idea of being a mum... it terrified her.

The smell of the piney air and sound of Sean returning made Bettie smile as she saw Sean walk up, sit next to her and pass her a black laptop. She hoped the answers she needed would be on the security cameras, which she didn't have access to but Graham did.

And after one passionate night between them, Graham had given her his passwords for anything she might need. At first she had made sure to forget them so Graham would never get in trouble, but Graham had unofficially cleared it with his boss.

The rule was as long as no one knew, Bettie had results and she didn't interfere with cases, it was okay.

Opening the laptop, Bettie clicked on a few buttons, swiped the mouse and tried to ignore the cold numbness that was starting to infect her fingers.

It didn't take long for her to access the security footage from a camera that looked at the house directly and Bettie played it, only to hear Sean laugh a little as they watched Bettie in her massive coat, thick trousers and messy hair go into the house.

As much as she was tempted to give Sean a gentle elbow in the ribs, she knew he was right. From this camera angle she hardly looked attractive and it was true. The camera definitely adds 10 pounds (or more likely 100 pounds for Bettie).

Bettie swiped the mouse a few more times as she fast forwarded the footage and there was no one there until Sean went into the house later on.

Cocking her head, Bettie tried to understand how this camera that had a wide open view of the house and most of the road didn't manage to see anyone come or go.

"Aunty, any other cameras?"

Bettie looked at the choice of cameras that the police had access to and there was only one other camera she could look at. She clicked on it, sped it up and smiled.

After a few moments of looking, Bettie found a

tall man wearing nothing more than a tracksuit, a black hat and black boots. Bettie stopped the footage and she zoomed in.

"Isn't that-" Sean said.

"Yes it is,"

Bettie recognised those boots, body and face anywhere. She never thought of Detective Inspector Lawrence as an attractive man but Bettie recognised his face anyway, and even his body was an odd shape, large in the chest, thin at the waist. All making it easy to identify on camera footage.

"What now Aunty?"

Bettie opened her mouth but she wasn't sure. She saw snow was starting to fall once more so she knew she had to be quick, she didn't want Sean driving in a snowstorm.

But what could she do?

Bettie knew she couldn't declare Lawrence guilty because the footage showed him going into a house and Bettie didn't need to check again to know who owned it, it was his own house. But there was something odd about it all.

"Could Graham use the footage?

Bettie shook her head. "I don't know but if Lawrence is the man who attacked me then-"

She remembered!

"Sean! I remember something about the man. I know it was a man for starters. He had a..." Bettie said as she did a circular motion on the back of her hands towards Sean.

"What? A tattoo? A Burn? A Cut?"

That was it.

"Yes a cut. Quite large. I remember it from when he was tying me up. I must have regained consciousness for a few seconds."

Sean nodded thoughtfully to himself.

"What?" Bettie asked.

Sean took out his phone. "In bed last night, me and Harry were looking at some of the pics from the ceremony,"

Bettie went to nod but she was a bit caught on the fact her nephew and his boyfriend were sleeping together.

Shaking those thoughts away and breathing in more of the piney air, Bettie took Sean's phone, looked at the ceremony's website and scrolled through the pictures.

She knew it wasn't a perfect idea as people only shook with their right hand but it was the best idea she had.

There were tons of photos. Bettie had no idea that there was an official photographer, then she remembered that skinny boy that was probably Lawrence's grandson taking photos. Bettie shook her head, she would have thought the police would pay for a proper photographer for an official awards ceremony.

"Here," Sean stopped Bettie scrolling and zoomed in on the photos of Lawrence shaking hands with the different police officers.

Bettie flicked through them, frowning as in each photo Lawrence's right hand was clear. But there was one photo with an officer with a broken right arm so Lawrence couldn't shake it. So he had to shake it with his left hand.

Sean zoomed in. "And we have it,"

Bettie smiled as she took a screenshot of the photo, edited it with a red circle and sent it to

Graham. There was a large cut in Lawrence's hand that was going to be his downfall.

***

A few hours later with her family talking, laughing and playing Christmas songs, Bettie allowed the soft sofa to take her weight as she sat down. For a moment Bettie just wanted a few seconds of peace so she focused on the amazing smells of Christmas pudding, cake and mince pies.

Her sister definitely knew how to make great mince pies, Bettie could almost taste their sweet fruitiness on her tongue.

Bettie looked around at all her amazing family from her tall beautiful nephew who saved her to her mini-helper Harry to her knight in shining armour, her beautiful Graham. They all sat on the sofa next to her and talked and laughed with each other.

Because it was that time of year.

It was the time of year for laughing, loving and joy and that's what they were doing here tonight. After what happened to Bettie, everyone wanted to have a practice (an excuse) Christmas dinner with all the trimmings and everything.

Bettie still thought it was an awful fuss over her just because she got kidnapped (again) and it was already past midnight. But then her nephew and sister reminded her that she was important to them, and she mattered.

As she listened to everything going on around her (and tried to ignore the crashing, banging and bubbling of her sister in the kitchen), Bettie stared at her beautiful Graham's face as she remembered how he told her about the official investigation that was launching into Lawrence and if she was willing to testify.

She was.

And so that case was done, Bettie wrapped her arms around her family and Graham as she knew she had proved Lawrence was corrupt, she had solved who kidnapped her and most importantly she had got to have a Christmas dinner early with the people she loved.

All because of a crime, Christmas and a closet.

MYSTERIOUS CHRISTMAS

GET YOUR FREE SHORT STORY NOW!
And get signed up to Connor Whiteley's newsletter to hear about new gripping books, offers and exciting projects. (You'll never be sent spam)

https://www.subscribepage.com/wintersignup

About the author:

Connor Whiteley is the author of over 60 books in the sci-fi fantasy, nonfiction psychology and books for writer's genre and he is a Human Branding Speaker and Consultant.

He is a passionate warhammer 40,000 reader, psychology student and author.

Who narrates his own audiobooks and he hosts The Psychology World Podcast.

All whilst studying Psychology at the University of Kent, England.

Also, he was a former Explorer Scout where he gave a speech to the Maltese President in August 2018 and he attended Prince Charles' 70th Birthday Party at Buckingham Palace in May 2018.

Plus, he is a self-confessed coffee lover!

Other books by Connor Whiteley:

Bettie English Private Eye Series
A Very Private Woman
The Russian Case
A Very Urgent Matter
A Case Most Personal
Trains, Scots and Private Eyes
The Federation Protects
Cops, Robbers and Private Eyes
Just Ask Bettie English
An Inheritance To Die For
The Death of Graham Adams
Bearing Witness
The Twelve
The Wrong Body
The Assassination Of Bettie English
Wining And Dying
Eight Hours
Uniformed Cabal
A Case Most Christmas

Gay Romance Novellas
Breaking, Nursing, Repairing A Broken Heart
Jacob And Daniel
Fallen For A Lie
Spying And Weddings
Clean Break

Awakening Love
Meeting A Country Man
Loving Prime Minister
Snowed In Love
Never Been Kissed
Love Betrays You

<u>Lord of War Origin Trilogy:</u>
Not Scared Of The Dark
Madness
Burn Them All

<u>The Fireheart Fantasy Series</u>
Heart of Fire
Heart of Lies
Heart of Prophecy
Heart of Bones
Heart of Fate

<u>City of Assassins (Urban Fantasy)</u>
City of Death
City of Martyrs
City of Pleasure
City of Power

Agents of The Emperor
Return of The Ancient Ones
Vigilance
Angels of Fire
Kingmaker
The Eight
The Lost Generation
Hunt
Emperor's Council
Speaker of Treachery
Birth Of The Empire
Terraforma
Spaceguard

The Rising Augusta Fantasy Adventure Series
Rise To Power
Rising Walls
Rising Force
Rising Realm

Lord Of War Trilogy (Agents of The Emperor)
Not Scared Of The Dark
Madness
Burn It All Down

Miscellaneous:
RETURN
FREEDOM
SALVATION
Reflection of Mount Flame
The Masked One
The Great Deer
English Independence

OTHER SHORT STORIES BY CONNOR WHITELEY

Mystery Short Story Collections
Criminally Good Stories Volume 1: 20 Detective Mystery Short Stories
Criminally Good Stories Volume 2: 20 Private Investigator Short Stories
Criminally Good Stories Volume 3: 20 Crime Fiction Short Stories
Criminally Good Stories Volume 4: 20 Science Fiction and Fantasy Mystery Short Stories
Criminally Good Stories Volume 5: 20 Romantic Suspense Short Stories

Mystery Short Stories:
Protecting The Woman She Hated
Finding A Royal Friend
Our Woman In Paris
Corrupt Driving
A Prime Assassination
Jubilee Thief
Jubilee, Terror, Celebrations
Negative Jubilation
Ghostly Jubilation
Killing For Womenkind
A Snowy Death
Miracle Of Death
A Spy In Rome
The 12:30 To St Pancreas
A Country In Trouble
A Smokey Way To Go
A Spicy Way To GO
A Marketing Way To Go
A Missing Way To Go
A Showering Way To Go
Poison In The Candy Cane
Kendra Detective Mystery Collection Volume 1
Kendra Detective Mystery Collection Volume 2
Mystery Short Story Collection Volume 1

Mystery Short Story Collection Volume 2
Criminal Performance
Candy Detectives
Key To Birth In The Past

All books in 'An Introductory Series':
Careers In Psychology
Psychology of Suicide
Dementia Psychology
Clinical Psychology Reflections Volume 4
Forensic Psychology of Terrorism And Hostage-Taking
Forensic Psychology of False Allegations
Year In Psychology
CBT For Anxiety
CBT For Depression
Applied Psychology
BIOLOGICAL PSYCHOLOGY 3RD EDITION
COGNITIVE PSYCHOLOGY THIRD EDITION
SOCIAL PSYCHOLOGY- 3RD EDITION
ABNORMAL PSYCHOLOGY 3RD EDITION
PSYCHOLOGY OF RELATIONSHIPS- 3RD EDITION
DEVELOPMENTAL PSYCHOLOGY 3RD

EDITION
HEALTH PSYCHOLOGY
RESEARCH IN PSYCHOLOGY
A GUIDE TO MENTAL HEALTH AND TREATMENT AROUND THE WORLD- A GLOBAL LOOK AT DEPRESSION
FORENSIC PSYCHOLOGY
THE FORENSIC PSYCHOLOGY OF THEFT, BURGLARY AND OTHER CRIMES AGAINST PROPERTY
CRIMINAL PROFILING: A FORENSIC PSYCHOLOGY GUIDE TO FBI PROFILING AND GEOGRAPHICAL AND STATISTICAL PROFILING.
CLINICAL PSYCHOLOGY
FORMULATION IN PSYCHOTHERAPY
PERSONALITY PSYCHOLOGY AND INDIVIDUAL DIFFERENCES
CLINICAL PSYCHOLOGY REFLECTIONS VOLUME 1
CLINICAL PSYCHOLOGY REFLECTIONS VOLUME 2
Clinical Psychology Reflections Volume 3
CULT PSYCHOLOGY
Police Psychology

www.ingramcontent.com/pod-product-compliance
Lightning Source LLC
LaVergne TN
LVHW011853060526
838200LV00054B/4313